Dear Parent:
Your child's love of reading starts here!

Every child learns to read in a different way and at his or her own speed. Some go back and forth between reading levels and read favorite books again and again. Others read through each level in order. You can help your young reader improve and become more confident by encouraging his or her own interests and abilities. From books your child reads with you to the first books he or she reads alone, there are I Can Read Books for every stage of reading:

SHARED READING
Basic language, word repetition, and whimsical illustrations, ideal for sharing with your emergent reader

BEGINNING READING
Short sentences, familiar words, and simple concepts for children eager to read on their own

READING WITH HELP
Engaging stories, longer sentences, and language play for developing readers

READING ALONE
Complex plots, challenging vocabulary, and high-interest topics for the independent reader

ADVANCED READING
Short paragraphs, chapters, and exciting themes for the perfect bridge to chapter books

I Can Read Books have introduced children to the joy of reading since 1957. Featuring award-winning authors and illustrators and a fabulous cast of beloved characters, I Can Read Books set the standard for beginning readers.

A lifetime of discovery begins with the magical words "I Can Read!"

Visit www.icanread.com for information
on enriching your child's reading experience.

Watercolor paints and a black pen were used for the full-color art.

HarperCollins®, ☕®, and I Can Read Book® are trademarks of HarperCollins Publishers.

Library of Congress Cataloging-in-Publication Data

Parish, Herman.
   Bravo, Amelia Bedelia! / by Herman Parish ; pictures by Lynn Sweat.
      p.   cm.—(An I can read book)
   "Greenwillow Books."
   Summary: From the time she is sent to pick up the guest conductor, Amelia Bedelia's normal confusion causes quite an uproar at the school concert.
    ISBN-10: 0-688-15154-X (trade bdg.) — ISBN-13: 978-0-688-15154-6 (trade bdg.)
    ISBN-10: 0-688-15155-8 (lib. bdg.) — ISBN-13: 978-0-688-15155-3 (lib. bdg.)
    ISBN-10: 0-06-444318-3 (pbk.) — ISBN-13: 978-0-06-444318-0 (pbk.)
    [1. Concerts—Fiction. 2. Humorous stories.] I. Sweat, Lynn, ill. II. Title.
PZ7.P2185 Br 1997   96-09589
[E]—dc20   CIP
                                                      AC

15 16 SCP 20 19 18 17

❖   Originally published by Greenwillow Books, an imprint of HarperCollins Publishers, in 1997.

For Rosemary,
my lova
—H.P.

For Jennifer
and Sarah
—L.S.

Bravo, Amelia Bedelia!

by Herman Parish

pictures by Lynn Sweat

HarperCollins*Publishers*

It was the day of the school concert.

Mrs. Rogers was very upset.

"Where is Amelia Bedelia?

I sent her to the station two hours ago

to pick up our new conductor.

The orchestra is waiting

to practice, and . . ."

"Yoo-hoo," said Amelia Bedelia.

"I'm back."

"Where is the conductor?"

said Mrs. Rogers.

"I told you to pick up the conductor."

"I tried my best," said Amelia Bedelia.

"But he was too big for me to pick up."

A large man in a blue uniform
followed Amelia Bedelia into the gym.
"Oh, no!" said Mrs. Rogers.
"This man isn't the conductor!"
"He sure is," said Amelia Bedelia.
"Look at his uniform."

"I did not mean a *train* conductor,"
said Mrs. Rogers.

"I meant a *musical* conductor."

"He is very musical,"
said Amelia Bedelia.

"He whistled all the way over here."

Just then a man

in a nice black suit

jogged into the gym.

"I am sorry I am so late," he said.

"No one met me at the station."

"The *real* conductor," said Mrs. Rogers.

"Thank goodness you are here."

"Look, lady," said the other conductor,

"I like music,

but I've got a train to catch."

"Catch a train!" said Amelia Bedelia.

"Be sure to use both hands.

Trains are heavy."

"Never mind," said Mrs. Rogers.

"I will drive him back to the station.

Amelia Bedelia,

you help the other conductor."

"Hurry back," said Amelia Bedelia.

"You do not want to miss the concert."

The conductor said hello
to the students. "Let's practice
a few numbers," he said.
He waved his baton to start the music.
"One, two, and *three*!"

Amelia Bedelia kept on counting:

"Four, five, and *six*!

Seven, eight, and . . ."

"Stop!" said the conductor.

"Did we practice enough numbers?"

asked Amelia Bedelia.

The children giggled.

"Don't count out loud,"

said the conductor.

"You can tap your toe, if you like."

Amelia Bedelia bent over

to reach her toes.

Tap, tap, *tap*! Tap, tap, *tap*!

The children began to laugh.

TAP, TAP, *TAP*!

went the conductor's baton.

"Quiet, please. We have to practice,"
the conductor said.

He waved his baton.

The orchestra began to play.

Amelia Bedelia was enjoying

the music until a bee flew in.

"Shoo!" said Amelia Bedelia.

"Go away!"

She tried to swat that bee.

She waved her arms around.

The conductor stopped the music.

"Miss Bedelia, *I* am the conductor.

Only *I* get to wave my arms around."

"Sorry," said Amelia Bedelia.

"There is a bee, see?"

"A-B-C?" asked the conductor.

"We are practicing music,

not the alphabet."

The orchestra started up again.

So did that bee.

"Excuse me," said Amelia Bedelia.

"May I borrow your pot lids?"

The boy laughed. "Sure. Here you go."

"Bye-bye, bee," said Amelia Bedelia.

Kee-RRRASH!

The music came to a halt.

"Miss Bedelia," shouted the conductor.

"We were playing a B-flat.

Would you call that a B-flat?"

Amelia Bedelia looked at the bee.

"Absolutely," said Amelia Bedelia.

"A bee couldn't get any flatter."

"So you read notes," said the conductor.

"Only if they are addressed to me,"

said Amelia Bedelia.

"Do you play?" asked the conductor.

"I play every day," said Amelia Bedelia.

"Mr. Rogers says

I'm an expert at fiddling."

The conductor handed her a violin.

"An expert fiddler," he said.

"Then you must play by ear."

"If you insist," said Amelia Bedelia.

She rubbed her ear across the strings.

"Ouch! Owie! Help!"

cried Amelia Bedelia.

A girl helped her untangle her hair.

"Expert fiddler indeed,"

said the conductor.

"Next time you should use a bow."

"I'll use ribbons and

barrettes, too," said Amelia Bedelia.

The conductor shook
his head.
"You should try
a different instrument."
"Which one?" asked Amelia Bedelia.
"Try the French horn,"
said the conductor.
"Or maybe another
wind instrument.
Or take up something
in the string section."

The audience began to come
into the gym.
It was almost time for the concert.
Amelia Bedelia looked sad.
"Is there something I could play today?"
asked Amelia Bedelia.

"Only this," said the conductor.

"Anyone can play the triangle."

Amelia Bedelia was so excited.

She hit the triangle very hard.

"Play it lower!" said the conductor.

Amelia Bedelia sat down on the floor.

"I give up," said the conductor.
"Just hit the triangle *once* after
the drum roll and when you hear this."
He signaled to a boy
to play the chimes.

"I'll get it," said Amelia Bedelia.

She ran for the nearest door.

"Come back here,"

said the conductor.

"Didn't you hear that doorbell?"

asked Amelia Bedelia.

"No one is at the door,"

said the conductor.

"When you hear those chimes,

you come in."

"That's easy," said Amelia Bedelia.

She opened the door and went out.

"Where are you going?"

said the conductor.

"I have to go out

before I can come in,"

said Amelia Bedelia.

She shut the door behind her.

"Good riddance!" said the conductor.

"I'll let her out

after the concert is over."

Every seat in the gym was filled.

Mrs. Rogers got back just in time.

"*Now* where has Amelia Bedelia gone?"

said Mrs. Rogers.

She introduced the conductor

to the audience.

He waved his baton

and the concert began.

Amelia Bedelia heard the music start.

"I must listen for when to come in,"

she said to herself.

She looked around the storeroom.

"While I wait, maybe I can find

those instruments he told me about.

Where would I find a string section'"

She picked up a piece of rope.

"This is the only string I see,"

said Amelia Bedelia.

"I'll cut off a section later."

Amelia Bedelia looked some more.

"Ah-ha! Wind instruments.

Should I try a big one or a little one?"

She took the little wind instrument.

"Where would they put a French horn?"

said Amelia Bedelia.

She sat down to think.

"YEOW!" she cried.

She looked where she had sat.

"Lucky me—I found *two* horns.

They may not be French, but they'll do."

"Whoops! There's that doorbell again,"
said Amelia Bedelia. "I'm late!"
She flung open the storeroom door.
"Gangway! I'm coming in!"

The cord from the wind instrument
got tangled in her legs.

"Watch out!" said Amelia Bedelia.

She fell into the big bass drum.

Baaa-BOoooom!

The drum began to roll.

It rolled right at the conductor.

"Stop!" he yelled. "I said *STOP*!"

It stopped . . . after it ran into him.

The conductor was very mad.

"You ruined my concert,

Amelia Bedelia!

What have you got to say for yourself?"

Amelia Bedelia didn't know what to say.

So she did what he had said to do.

She hit the triangle once.

DING!

All the students

began to clap and cheer.

"What a cool concert," said a boy.

"I want to play in the orchestra,"

said a girl.

"Me, too!" said each and every one.

The conductor pulled Amelia Bedelia
out of the drum.

"Was that a good drum roll?"
asked Amelia Bedelia.

"You played it by ear,"
said the conductor.

"I used my whole body,"
said Amelia Bedelia.

Everyone was
standing up
and clapping.
The conductor
and Amelia Bedelia
took a bow.

"My gracious!" said Mrs. Rogers.

"Are you hurt, Amelia Bedelia?"

"I had fun," said Amelia Bedelia.

"But I'd rather fiddle around at home."

"*That* is music to my ears,"

said the conductor.

The next day Amelia Bedelia made
a "thank you" note for the conductor.
She forgot to sign it.
But somehow the conductor knew
that it was from Amelia Bedelia.

Read all the books about
Amelia Bedelia

Amelia Bedelia

Thank You, Amelia Bedelia

Amelia Bedelia and the Surprise Shower

Come Back, Amelia Bedelia

Play Ball, Amelia Bedelia

Teach Us, Amelia Bedelia

Good Work, Amelia Bedelia

Amelia Bedelia Helps Out

Amelia Bedelia and the Baby

Amelia Bedelia Goes Camping

Merry Christmas, Amelia Bedelia

Amelia Bedelia's Family Album

Good Driving, Amelia Bedelia

Amelia Bedelia 4 Mayor

Calling Doctor Amelia Bedelia

Amelia Bedelia, Bookworm

Happy Haunting, Amelia Bedelia

Amelia Bedelia, Rocket Scientist?

Amelia Bedelia Under Construction